EDWARD AND GORDON

by

The Rev. W. Awdry

with illustrations by
C. Reginald Dalby

Grolier

Edward's Day Out

ONCE upon a time there was a little engine called Edward. He lived in a shed with five other engines. They were all bigger than Edward and boasted about it. "The driver won't choose you again," they said. "He wants big, strong engines like us." Edward had not been out for a long time; he began to feel sad.

Just then the driver and fireman came along to start work.

The driver looked at Edward. "Why are you sad?" he asked. "Would you like to come out today?"

"Yes, please," said Edward. So the fireman lit the fire and made a nice lot of steam.

Then the driver pulled the lever, and Edward puffed away.

"Peep, peep," he whistled. "Look at me now."

The others were very cross at being left behind.

Away went Edward to get some coaches.

"Be careful, Edward," said the coaches, "don't bump and bang us like the other engines do." So Edward came up to the coaches, very, very gently, and the shunter fastened the coupling.

"Thank you, Edward," said the coaches. "That was kind, we are glad you are taking us today."

Then they went to the station where the people were waiting.

"Peep, peep," whistled Edward—"get in quickly, please."

So the people got in quickly and Edward waited happily for the guard to blow his whistle, and wave his green flag.

He waited and waited—there was no whistle, no green flag. "Peep, peep, peep, peep— where is that guard?" Edward was getting anxious.

The driver and fireman asked the Station-Master, "Have you seen the guard?" "No," he said. They asked the porter, "Have you seen the guard?" "Yes—last night," said the porter.

Edward began to get cross. "Are we ever going to start?" he said.

Just then a little boy shouted, "Here he comes!" and there the guard was, running down the hill with his flags in one hand and a sandwich in the other.

He ran on to the platform, blew his whistle, and jumped into his van.

Edward puffed off. He did have a happy day. All the children ran to wave as he went past and he met old friends at all the stations. He worked so hard that the driver promised to take him out again next day.

"I'm going out again tomorrow," he told the other engines that night in the shed. "What do you think of that?"

But he didn't hear what they thought, for he was so tired and happy that he fell asleep at once.

Edward and Gordon

ONE of the engines in Edward's shed was called Gordon. He was very big and very proud.

"You watch me this afternoon, little Edward," he boasted, "as I rush through with the Express; that will be a splendid sight for you."

Just then his driver pulled the lever. "Good-bye, little Edward," said Gordon, as he puffed away, "look out for me this afternoon!"

Edward went off, too, to do some shunting.

Edward liked shunting. It was fun playing with trucks. He would come up quietly and give them a pull.

"Oh! Oh! Oh! Oh! Oh!" screamed the trucks. "Whatever is happening?"

Then he would stop and the silly trucks would go bump into each other. "Oh! Oh! Oh! Oh!" they cried again.

Edward pushed them until they were running nicely, and when they weren't expecting it he would stop; one of them would be sure to run on to another line. Edward played till there were no more trucks; then he stopped to rest.

Presently he heard a whistle. Gordon came puffing along, very slowly, and very crossly. Instead of nice shining coaches, he was pulling a lot of very dirty coal trucks.

"A goods train! a goods train! a goods train!" he grumbled. "The shame of it, the shame of it, the shame of it."

He went slowly through, with the trucks clattering and banging behind him.

Edward laughed, and went to find some more trucks.

Soon afterwards a porter came and spoke to his driver. "Gordon can't get up the hill. Will you take Edward and push him, please?"

They found Gordon half-way up the hill and very cross. His driver and fireman were talking to him severely. "You are not trying!" they told him.

"I can't do it," said Gordon. "The noisy trucks hold an engine back so. If they were coaches now—clean sensible things that come quietly—that would be different."

Edward's driver came up. "We've come to push," he said.

"No use at all," said Gordon.

"You wait and see," said Edward's driver.

They brought the train back to the bottom of the hill. Edward came up behind the brake-van ready to push.

"Peep, peep, I'm ready," said Edward.

"Poop, poop, no good," grumbled Gordon.

The guard blew his whistle and they pulled and pushed as hard as they could.

"I can't do it, I can't do it, I can't do it," puffed Gordon.

"I will do it, I will do it, I will do it," puffed Edward.

"I can't do it, I will do it, I can't do it, I will do it, I can't do it, I will do it," they puffed together.

Edward pushed and puffed and puffed and pushed, as hard as ever he could, and almost before he realized it, Gordon found himself at the top of the hill.

"I've done it! I've done it! I've done it!" he said proudly, and forgot all about Edward pushing behind. He didn't wait to say "Thank you", but ran on so fast that he passed two stations before his driver could make him stop.

Edward had pushed so hard that when he got to the top he was out of breath.

Gordon ran on so fast that Edward was left behind.

The guard waved and waved, but Edward couldn't catch up.

He ran on to the next station, and there the driver and fireman said they were very pleased with him. The fireman gave him a nice long drink of water, and the driver said, "I'll get out my paint tomorrow, and give you a beautiful new coat of blue with red stripes, then you'll be the smartest engine in the shed."

This book club edition published by Grolier 1994

Published by arrangement with Reed Children's Books
First published in Great Britain 1945 as part of *The Railway Series* No. 1.
Copyright © William Heinemann Ltd. 1945.
This edition copyright © William Heinemann Ltd. 1994